FUNNY JOKES

FOR

9

YEAR OLD KIDS

HUNDREDS OF HILARIOUS JOKES INSIDE!

JIMMY JONES

Hundreds of really funny, hilarious jokes that will have the kids in fits of laughter in no time!

They're all in here - the funniest
- Jokes
- Riddles
- Tongue Twisters
- Knock Knock Jokes

for 9 year old kids!

Funny kids love funny jokes and this brand new collection of original and classic jokes promises hours of fun for the whole family!

Books by Jimmy Jones

Funny Jokes For Funny Kids
Knock Knock Jokes For Funny Kids

Funny Jokes For Kids Series
All Ages 5 -12!

To see all the latest books by
Jimmy Jones just go to
kidsjokebooks.com

Contents

Funny Jokes! 5

Funny Knock Knock Jokes! 34

Funny Riddles! 64

Funny Tongue Twisters! 76

Bonus Funny Jokes! 84

Bonus Knock Knock Jokes! 96

Thank you so much 108

Funny Jokes!

Which superhero is good at serving icecream?

ScooperMan!

Why was the computer teacher scared?

She saw a mouse!

Why are baby cows so cute?

They are adora-bull!

Why did the cow go to yoga class?
To be more flexi-bull!

Why couldn't the aliens get a park on the moon?
It was full!

What is grey, has a trunk and four legs?
A mouse going on vacation!

Why don't corn cobs fly on planes?
Their ears pop!

Why do golfers wear 3 pairs of pants?
In case they get a hole in one!

Why did the strawberry look so sad?
It was a blue berry!

If a king was only 12 inches tall, what would you call him?

A ruler!

What do you get if you cross a rooster with a poodle?

A CockaPoodleDoo!

What happens if you throw some butter out the window?

You see a butterfly!

What did the small light bulb say to the big light bulb?

Watts up?

Why was 6 really scared of 7?

7, 8, 9!

What is a chicken's favorite vegetable?

Broc, broc, broc, broccoli!

How did the banana leave work early?

He split!

How did the frog feel when she hurt her leg?

Un-hoppy!

What did the doctor say to the patient with double vision?

Close one eye!

Why do bakers go to banks?
To get more dough!

What did the dad potato name his son?
Chip!

Which bird recycles?
A Two-can!

What do you call an elephant that didn't have a bath for a year?

A smellyphant!

What did the policeman say to the robber snowman?

Freeze!

What happens if you cross a computer and a life guard?

You get a screensaver!

Why was the dog on the ice at the hockey game?

He was the Ruffaree!

What happened to the cat that ate 3 lemons?

She became a sour puss!

Where did the T-Rex buy a birthday gift?

The dino-store!

What sort of dog really loves bubble baths?
Shampoodles!

Why did the shoe go on a date?
To find her sole mate!

What do frogs eat on really hot days?
Hop-sicles!

How did the dog stop the video from playing?

By pressing the paws button!

Why did the toilet go to hospital?

It was feeling a bit flushed!

What is the best time for a big storm?

Mon-soon!

Why did the boy love sharks?
He was a fin-atic!

What did the crab say to the big wave?
Long time no sea!

What happened when the elephant ate a computer?
He had lots of memory!

What did one coin say to the other coin?
Together, we make cents!

Why did the restaurant on the moon close?
It had no atmosphere!

What do you call a very rich elf?
Welfy!

What did the bees do when they moved into their new house?

Had a house swarming party!

Why was the broom late for work at the factory?

He overswept!

Why did Mickey Mouse hire a rental car?

So he could drive a Minnie van!

Why did the duck cross the road?
To prove she wasn't chicken!

How do snowmen get to work?
On their icicle!

How did the math teacher know the girl was lying?
Her story didn't add up!

What is a birds favorite month?
Flock-Tober!

What kept the cavemen awake at night?
A Dino-Snore!

What do you do when a dinosaur sneezes?
Get covered in boogers!

What did the grumpy doctor lose his job?
He lost his patients!

What do you call a polar bear in the desert?
Lost!

What happens when 2 silkworms have a race?
It ends in a tie!

Why was the chicken student sad?
She failed her eggsams!

Why are graveyards so noisy?
Because of all of the coffin!

What TV shows do you watch in the kitchen?
Soup operas!

What did the leopard say after lunch?
That really hit the spots!

What exercise do cats do in the morning?
Puss Ups!

Why did everyone trust the caveman?
He was a caveman of his word!

What did the can of soda study at college?
Fizzics!

What do ghosts like for dinner?
Gumboo!

Who is the master of the pencil case?
The ruler!

Why did the jogger eat an apple pie?
She liked puff pastry!

Where did the ghost go on her vacation?
The dead sea!

Which dinosaur spoke English and knew all the words?
The thesaurus!

What do you call a train that sneezes?
Ah Choo Choo!

What do you call a fairy who hasn't had a
shower for 3 weeks?
Stinker Bell!

Why are beavers always on the internet?
They never log off!

Why was the boy standing on a clock?
He wanted to be on time!

Which city building usually has the most stories?
The library!

Why did the chicken love her little sister?
She was a good egg!

Why do owls love going to parties?
They are always such a hoot!

Which is the wealthiest bird?
The ost-rich!

What did the thief get after he stole a calendar?
12 months!

Why do bees hum?
They don't know the words!

What did the old tornado say to his wife?
Let's twist again! Like we did last summer!

What fruit do vampires love?
Necktarines!

Which birds like to kneel down?
Birds of prey!

Where do fish sleep?
In their river bed!

What was the fake noodle's Secret Agent name?
The Impasta!

What was a better invention than the first telephone?

The second telephone!

What was the apple doing at the gym?

Working on his core!

Why did the boy take 3 rolls of toilet paper to the birthday party?

He was a party pooper!

Why was Cyclops no good as a teacher?
He only had one pupil!

Where did the bee go to the toilet?
The BP station!

How did the swim team get to practice?
They carpooled!

What did the Queen do when she burped?
Issued a royal pardon!

What is an Oak tree's favorite cold drink?
Root beer!

Why was the math book sad and grumpy?
It had so many problems!

Funny Knock Knock Jokes!

Knock knock.

Who's there?

Thor.

Thor who?

My hand is Thor from all this knocking!

Knock knock.

Who's there?

Disguise.

Disguise who?

Disguise the limit!

Knock knock.

Who's there?

Quiet Tina.

Quiet Tina who?

Quiet Tina Library!

I'm trying to read!

Knock knock.

Who's there?

Freeze.

Freeze who?

Freeze a jolly good fellowwww!

Knock knock.

Who's there?

CD.

Cd who?

CD big clouds? It's gonna rain!

Knock knock.

Who's there?

Tweet.

Tweet who?

Would you like tweet an apple?

They are really tasty!

Knock knock.

Who's there?

Lefty.

Lefty who?

Lefty key at home so I had to knock!

Knock knock.

Who's there?

Juicy.

Juicy who?

Juicy the news! Our team won! Yay!

Knock knock.

Who's there?

Taco.

Taco who?

I want to Taco bout why your bell doesn't work!

Knock knock.

Who's there?

Stew.

Stew who?

Stew early to go home!

Let's go to the park!

Knock knock.

Who's there?

Omelet.

Omelet who?

Omelet shorter than you so I can't reach the bell!

Knock knock.

Who's there?

Cereal.

Cereal who?

Cereal pleasure to meet you today my good sir!

Knock knock.

Who's there?

Kent.

Kent who?

Kent you see I want to come in!

I've been waiting for 3 hours!

Knock knock.

Who's there?

Hawaii.

Hawaii who?

Great thanks, Hawaii you?

Knock knock.

Who's there?

Terrain.

Terrain who?

It's starting terrain, do you have an umbrella?

Knock knock.

Who's there?

Les.

Les who?

Les go to the beach while it's still sunny!

Knock knock.

Who's there?

Obi wan.

Obi wan who?

Obi Wan of your best friends! Let me in!

Knock knock.

Who's there?

Riot.

Riot who?

I'm Riot on time so let's go!

Knock knock.

Who's there?

Waiter.

Waiter who?

Waiter I tell your mom!

You're in trouble now!

Knock knock.

Who's there?

Wire.

Wire who?

Wire we talking through this door?

Open up already!

Knock knock.

Who's there?

Window.

Window who?

Window we start holidays? I think it's next week! Yay!

Knock knock.

Who's there?

Colin.

Colin who?

Colin all cars! Colin all cars! Emergency!

Knock knock.

Who's there?

Ice cream.

Ice cream who?

Ice cream when I jump in the pool!

It's fun!

Knock knock.

Who's there?

Chicken.

Chicken who?

Better Chicken the oven!

Something is burning!

Knock knock.

Who's there?

Amy.

Amy who?

Amy fraid I can't remember!

Knock knock.

Who's there?

Needle.

Needle who?

Needle hand to move your TV?

I've got big muscles!

Knock knock.

Who's there?

Ozzie.

Ozzie who?

Ozzie you later on, dude!

Knock knock.

Who's there?

Jester.

Jester who?

Jester second!

Why are you in my house?

Knock knock.

Who's there?

Java.

Java who?

Java cup of sugar for my mom?

Knock knock.

Who's there?

Taco.

Taco who?

I would like to taco 'bout our range of doorbells. Do you have a minute sir?

Knock knock.

Who's there?

Ears.

Ears who?

Ears another funny joke!

Knock knock.

Who's there?

Dale.

Dale who?

Dale be comin' 'round the mountain

when dey come!

Knock knock.

Who's there?

Mushroom.

Mushroom who?

Do you have mushroom left in the car?

Knock knock.

Who's there?

Mint.

Mint who?

I mint to tell you - You're doorbell is broken!

Knock knock.

Who's there?

Nose.

Nose who?

I Nose plenty more Knock knock jokes for you!

Knock knock.

Who's there?

Toad.

Toad who?

I toad you these jokes would be really funny!

Knock knock.

Who's there?

Butter.

Butter who?

I Butter hurry up and come inside!

Knock knock.

Who's there?

Guess Simon.

Guess Simon who?

Guess Simon the wrong place!

Sorry to disturb you madam!

Knock knock.

Who's there?

Tank.

Tank who?

You're very welcome sir!

Knock knock.

Who's there?

Fanny.

Fanny who?

Fanny body home?

Why don't you answer?

Knock knock.

Who's there?

Howl.

Howl who?

Howl you know if you don't ever open up this door!

Knock knock.

Who's there?

Keith.

Keith who?

Keith me now my one true love!

Knock knock.

Who's there?

Orange.

Orange who?

Orange you glad I finally made it?

Sorry I'm late!

Knock knock.

Who's there?

Aloha.

Aloha who?

Aloha bell would be handy because

then I could reach it!

Knock knock.

Who's there?

Walrus.

Walrus who?

Why do you walrus ask me that?

Knock knock.

Who's there?

Zinc.

Zinc who?

I zinc you are a very nice person!

Knock knock.

Who's there?

Renata.

Renata who?

Renata sugar! Do you have any?

Knock knock.

Who's there?

Tex.

Tex who?

Tex so long to open this door!

Please give me a key!

Knock knock.

Who's there?

Stopwatch.

Stopwatch who?

Stopwatch you're doing and let me in!

Knock knock.

Who's there?

Hannah.

Hannah who?

Hannah one and a two and a three and a four!

Knock knock.

Who's there?

Four eggs.

Four eggs who?

Four eggs-ample why don't you get a doorbell?

Knock knock.

Who's there?

Ben.

Ben who?

Ben knocking so long my hand feels like it's going to fall off!

Knock knock.

Who's there?

Van.

Van who?

Van are you going to let me in?

I'm hungry!

Knock knock.

Who's there?

Waa.

Waa who?

You sure are excited considering all I

did was knock!

Knock knock.

Who's there?

Honey bee.

Honey bee who?

Honey bee kind and open the door for your grandma!

Knock knock.

Who's there?

Athena.

Athena who?

Athena bear in your house so RUN!!!!!

Knock knock.

Who's there?

Zany.

Zany who?

Zany body home today? Let me in!

Knock knock.

Who's there?

Alden.

Alden who?

When you're Alden with your homework, let's go fishing!

Knock knock.

Who's there?

Noah.

Noah who?

Noah good place for a pizza?

I'm really hungry!

Knock knock.

Who's there?

Gopher.

Gopher who?

Gopher help quick! I think I broke

my leg! Owwww!

Funny Riddles!

Has anyone ever seen a catfish?
Yes, but they don't catch anything!

How can you unlock an ancient tomb?
Use a skeleton key!

What can you measure even though
sometimes it flies?
Time!

If we breathe oxygen in the daytime what do we breathe at night?

Nitrogen!

What has eyes but cannot see?

A potato!

What side of a bird has the most feathers?

The outside!

What is always taken before you get it?
Your photo!

What do you call a ketchup bottle in space?
A flying saucer!

Which fish comes out after a big storm?
A rainbow trout!

What do sheep watch on TV?
Flock-umentaries!

Which bird can lift the most weight?
The crane!

What holds water but has many holes?
A sponge!

How can you have a shower without using water?

Have a baby shower!

What has hands but can't touch anything?

A clock!

What is the main difference between a bird and a fly?

A bird can fly but a fly can't bird!

Why is hot faster than cold?
It's easy to catch a cold!

Which side of the house is the best place for the porch?
The outside!

What do you call a rodent's carpet?
A mouse mat!

What runs around a field but never moves?
A fence!

What are little, tiny baby crabs called?
Nippers!

What always hears but never talks?
Your ear!

What never speaks back unless spoken to?
An echo!

What do skunks say if the wind changes direction?
It's all coming back to me now!

What sort of fish is in every shoe?
An eel!

What type of lion is good in your garden?
A Dandelion!

What do you call a poodle covered in snow?
A chilli dog!

Where does Friday come before Thursday?
In the dictionary!

What goes up and down but doesn't move?
Stairs!

What has keys but no doors?
A piano!

What is the best type of haircut for a bee?
A buzz cut!

Which type of cow lives in an igloo?
An eskimooo!

Which snake is good at math?
The Pi-thon!

How many apples can you put into an empty bag?
One. Now it's not empty!

Which animal can you use to write a letter?
A pen-guin!

How can you tell where a train has come from?
By its tracks!

What key do you get at Christmas?
A tur-key!

Funny Tongue Twisters!

Tongue Twisters are great fun!
Start off slow.
How fast can you go?

Blow blue bubbles.
Blow blue bubbles.
Blow blue bubbles.

Shoe section.
Shoe section.
Shoe section.

Fred fed Ted bread.
Fred fed Ted bread.
Fred fed Ted bread.

Baboon bamboo.
Baboon bamboo.
Baboon bamboo.

Which wrist watch?
Which wrist watch?
Which wrist watch?

Crisp crusts crackle.
Crisp crusts crackle.
Crisp crusts crackle.

Watching washing.
Watching washing.
Watching washing.

Which witch wishes?
Which witch wishes?
Which witch wishes?

Clean clam can.
Clean clam can.
Clean clam can.

Bubble blubber trouble.
Bubble blubber trouble.
Bubble blubber trouble.

Three free throws.
Three free throws.
Three free throws.

Freeze flying fleas.
Freeze flying fleas.
Freeze flying fleas.

Please place peanuts.
Please place peanuts.
Please place peanuts.

Six sly shrimps.
Six sly shrimps.
Six sly shrimps.

Red lorry, yellow lorry
Red lorry, yellow lorry
Red lorry, yellow lorry

Butter brown bread.
Butter brown bread.
Butter brown bread.

Six sleek swans swam swiftly south.
Six sleek swans swam swiftly south.
Six sleek swans swam swiftly south.

Grow glowing grapes.
Grow glowing grapes.
Grow glowing grapes.

Three fleas fly.
Three fleas fly.
Three fleas fly.

Three free trees.
Three free trees.
Three free trees.

Crush grapes, grapes crush, crush grapes.
Crush grapes, grapes crush, crush grapes.
Crush grapes, grapes crush, crush grapes.

Swan swam over the sea.
Swan swam over the sea.
Swan swam over the sea.

She flosses fast.
She flosses fast.
She flosses fast.

Bonus Funny Jokes!

What is the best lunch in the desert?
A sandwich!

What do you call an alligator who eats Mars Bars?
A chocho-dile!

What do you call lamb covered in chocholate?
A Candy BAAAA!

If a deer costs one dollar, what is it?
A buck!

Why did the ghost catch a cold?
He got chilled to the bone!

If a monkey exploded, what sound would it make?
Baboom!

What did the snowman eat for his breakfast?

Frosted Flakes!

What do horses eat for a snack?

Hay-Zelnuts!

Why did the snail have a day off work?

He felt a bit sluggish!

What did the wasp throw in the park?
A fris-bee!

What is the best place for an elephant to store her luggage?
In her trunk!

What did the doctor say to the patient who told him he broke his leg in 2 places?
Stop going to those places!

What is a good dessert for a ghost?
I Scream and Booberry pie!

Why did the turkey cross the road?
Miss Chicken had the day off!

Why didn't the boy like the wooden car
with the wooden engine?
It wooden go!

Why was the glow worm looking sad?
His kids weren't very bright!

Where did the frog leave his coat?
In the croakroom!

What was the boy always late for school?
They kept ringing the bell before he got there!

What do you call a belt with a built in watch?

A waist of time!

What did the poodle say to his brother?

I have a bone to pick with you!

What time is it when an elephant sits on your lunch box?

Time to get a new lunch box!

Why did the pig get a second job?
He had to bring home the bacon!

What do you call a bell that falls into the pool?
Wringing wet!

What is the busiest time to go to the dentist?
Tooth hurty! (2.30)

Why was the spider hanging out on the computer?

He was making a website!

Why was the girl's homework in her dad's writing?

She borrowed his pen!

What did Mrs Claus say to Santa Claus when she looked out the window?

It looks like rain. dear!

What did the cannon name his son?
A son of a gun!

How did the first flying monkey get to work?
In her hot air baboon!

Why was the didgeridoo at the office?
To answer the phone if the

boomerang!

What did the lawyers say to the dentist?

Make sure you tell the tooth, the whole tooth and nothing but the tooth?

Why are triangles good at playing basketball?

They get three pointers!

Which puzzle makes you more angry the more you do it?

A Crossword puzzle!

What game did the Brontosaurus play with the caveman?

Squash!

Who did Dracula fall in love with?

The girl necks door!

Which dinosaur just broke up with his girlfriend?

The Tyrannosaurus Ex!

Bonus

Knock Knock Jokes!

Knock knock.

Who's there?

Adam.

Adam who?

Up and Adam! Time to go!

Knock knock.

Who's there?

Toucan.

Toucan who?

Toucan play that sort of game!

Knock knock.

Who's there?

Candy.

Candy who?

Candy owner of the dog come outside.

It won't stop barking!

Knock knock.

Who's there?

Ivor.

Ivor who?

Ivor you open the door or I will climb

through the window!

Knock knock.

Who's there?

Kenya.

Kenya who?

Kenya guess who is coming to my place for dinner?

Knock knock.

Who's there?

Hijack.

Hijack who?

Hi Jack, is Jill home?

Knock knock.

Who's there?

Randy.

Randy who?

Randy marathon yesterday!

I need new shoes!

Knock knock.

Who's there?

Sister.

Sister who?

Sister right place for the party tonight?

Knock knock.

Who's there?

House.

House who?

House about we go to the mall?

Let's go!

Knock knock.

Who's there?

Jethro.

Jethro who?

Jethro a rope out the window and I'll

climb up!

Knock knock.

Who's there?

Olive.

Olive who?

Olive you lots and lots you know!

Knock knock.

Who's there?

Thermos.

Thermos who?

Thermos be a quicker way to open this door!

Knock knock.

Who's there?

Felix.

Felix who?

Felix my ice cream one more time he can buy me a new one!

Knock knock.

Who's there?

Alpaca.

Alpaca who?

Alpaca my bags in the morning and be on my way!

Knock knock.

Who's there?

Doris.

Doris who?

Doris a bit squeaky!

I think you need to oil it!

Knock knock.

Who's there?

Paula.

Paula who?

Paula door open and you will see!

Knock knock.

Who's there?

Dingo.

Dingo who?

Dingo anywhere yesterday!

Knock knock.

Who's there?

Carlotta.

Carlotta who?

Carlotta trouble when it breaks down!

Knock knock.

Who's there?

Cook.

Cook who?

Are you a cuckoo clock?

Knock knock.

Who's there?

Pudding.

Pudding who?

I'm pudding on my best dress for dinner! Do you like it?

Knock knock.

Who's there?

Ketchup.

Ketchup who?

Let's ketchup later on and have an icecream!

Knock knock.

Who's there?

Mabel.

Mabel who?

Mabel works but yours is broken.

Ha Ha!

Knock knock.

Who's there?

Cher.

Cher who?

Cher would like to come in before it gets dark!

Knock knock.

Who's there?

Mustache.

Mustache who?

I mustache you a question. Where were you on the night of the 15th?

Thank you so much

For reading our book.

I hope you have enjoyed these funny jokes for 9 year old kids as much as my kids and I did as we were putting this book together.

We really had a lot of fun and laughter creating and compiling this book and we really appreciate you for reading our book.

If you could possibly let us know what you thought of our book by way of a review we would really appreciate it 😊

To see all our latest books or leave a review just go to
kidsjokebooks.com
Once again, thanks so much for reading.

All the best,
Jimmy Jones
And also Ella & Alex (the kids)
And even Obi (the dog – he's very cute!)